Evincepub
Publishing

Evincepub Publishing

Nehru Nagar, Bilaspur, Chhattisgarh 495001
First Published by Evincepub Publishing
2021 Copyright © Mahwish khan 2021
All Rights Reserved.
ISBN: 978-93-5446-156-9

Mi Carazon

My heart

By
Mahwish khan

ABOUT THE BOOK

She left him because she loved him too much. He loved her so much that it became his passion . she became his reason to live Both of them loved , got betrayed and fought with there destiny to be together Witness The journey of love , passion and heartaches as bakht shah and kabir jahan witness the rollercoaster ride of there relationship and changing dynamics with the hilarious group of there friends Will love conquer it all?

ABOUT THE AUTHOR

Born in rajasthan mahwish khan always wanted to be different starting from the fact that despite being from science background she loved literature with all her heart. Wrote her first story on Wattpad and over a year earned love of more than three thousand peoples. Publishing her first book on her father's birthday because for mahwish her father is her inspiration, her hero.

PROLOGUE

Qatar

In the pitch black room seated the boss of Qatar

5 years … These last 5 years had changed the living perspective of kabir jahan

He's now only boss … The king of mobsters and a dreaded cold hearted mafia

Tapping his polished black shoe he was waiting for louis his first in command to gave him the information On the count of 5 his phone rang making him stop his moments

Hello! Louis voice was sounding amused as well as surprised

Boss …Anderson is dead

Kabir raised an eyebrow …. Any clue?

Boss again …the killer had left a j sign

Ok …with that he cut the call …in last 5 years all people that were his rivals or were after his family or her   They have been killed by this J who is still unknown to his eyes These murders mostly happen at night and next day the person just vanish leaving his sign that is J

Taking his cigar he blew a smoke looking at the cream walls of his room

They are just like him …lifeless!

Dubai

Ok aunty now slowly bend ..adjusting her glasess bakht

polietly instructed the lady she was treating   After
checking her up she checked her phone

Shoot … I am dead   that you are and because of you I
am late too you hobo! take a ryt and fudge off! She often
talks with her inner self … weird? That's bakht shah

She reached her apartment and saw her brother lying on
sofa with his legs on sham's face both were snoring
Rolling her eyes at there sleeping position bakht kicked
shams her brother

No reply

This men sleeps like dead she murmered and again kicked
him   But no avail

There they are sleeping alas I bought pizza .. she
announced than smirked and count

3

2

Good morning sister .. when did you came shams grinned
but than frown

Am I lying in a gutter? He cringed but than squeeled like
a girl jumping on a sleeping sahil

What? Are we thrown off the bed? Said a yawning sahil
Your sock claded feet was on my face and I choked to
death .. what if I had died without being a married men
HEAVENS! shams screeched dramatically

You won't die easily brother … Sahil consoled his twin
who was still horrified at his imaginations of being dead

Bakht rolled her eyes at her brothers and picked a cushion
and smacked there heads

Get up lazy asess and do the dishes Now! She ordered and
went to her room

Shams and sahil look at each other and made cry face

No this can't be happening!.

x

Shams dramatically cried looking at the movie while his twin again yawned still sleepy

Let's wash dishes otherwise she will throw us out and we won't be able to eat that delicious pasta I had stored in refrigerator .. sahil whispered to his twin

Dishes and bitches! Here we go …

Opening her wardrobe bakht was bombarded with piles of clothes

Are u alive in there? Should I come in?

What are u? A spiderman who will save me ? Bakht roll her eyes on her friend aka her subconscious inner self

Finally getting her nightwear she changed in it and went to dinner

So? Are we going doha than? Shams looked at his sister grinning showing his mouth which is full of food

 Yukkk … Eat like humans!

 Bakht threw a tissue on him

Should I start the packing? Sahil said making puppy face

Ofcourse bro n keep those sneakers they are my lucky charm u know … Shams suggested seriously as if discussing the economy making sahil nod obediently

Sighing bakht look at the two idiots n smiled

The only source of happiness in her life is these two

Meanwhile , doha

Uhu …Fahad groaned in his sleep feeling some heavy thing on himself

That thing jumped on him making him jolt up

A 7 month pregnant zoya grinned looking at her husband who is apparently scowling

Zee u are not a kid Fahad said rolling his eyes making zoya pout

I need icecream she said making baby face

 No was his reply

But …plz …she said again pouting

Her husband gave her a bored look instead .. sugars are not good for u

Plzzz .. she made a puppy face

Should I call Kabir … He used his last threat n that did the work

 Good night

Fahad chuckled shaking his head …. Pregnant zoya is 10× of previous one

Only she or kabir could handle her easily ..

Well If only she was here

 If only !

TABLE OF CONTENTS

Chapter 1

————◆————

Bakht looked out of the plane the clouds looking so calm to her eyes

She looked at her right where her brothers were sound asleep

They are going to stay with her friend amy and her sister

She closed her eyes …this is the first time in last 5 yrs she is going out of dubai

After coming back from Russia …

Russia

One word many emotions are related to that place She shook her head to eliminate those past memories that still haunt her

Taking deep breaths she plugged her earpods to distract her mind

Shams looked around with his aviaters turning heads of girls

And why not? He is one fine handsome specie afterall

But , he is not searching for a nice girl he is searching for a nice food stall

Sahil yawned on shams facemaking the boy squeel in disgust

No noise pollution shams said glaring sahil who ignored him

Bakht spotted amy and waved at her …

Hellooooooo ….amy came running to bakht shouting making people gave her looks

She jumped on bakht who lost balance and fell with a growl

Both girls land on floor with a thud …amy grinned still enthusiastic while bakht was looking a nice place to die

Hii baby boo …amy greeted bakht with her wiered Nick name making bakht roll her eyes

Hi to u too amy …can we get up …I am not that much comfortable on floor she sweetly smiled at amy who ignored her sarcasm

Hii .. I am Sahil her dear brother you can call me with a love name …

Before he could say more shams butt in ..

Noone calls him with love tho! Shams stated seriously making amy laugh

U are awesome …she said to shams who frown

No … I am shams …he corrected her with poker face making amy burst in laughter

Ohh god …babyboo ur bros are legit cute amy gush over boys who blushed making bakht scoff

Done with blushing? …bakht taunted her brothers who were shying like a new bride

Welcome to Doha. …sitting in car amy screamed making bakht almost jump out   She
has got wiered friends

As if you are normal … And
a wiered subconscious

Meanwhile.

Kabir came out of his mansion and took the car keys from driver

Today he is feeling really restless and hence wants to spend some time …alone without anyone around not even the driver

He start his range rover and headed to his office but …

The car seemed to be out of control

The breaks were fail …he punched the steering

Someone did this on purpose…

He immediately dialled louis number to inform him but before he could do anything

A long trolly followed by gunshots attacked the car making it roll over the road

Doctor? It's been 12 fucking hours can u tell me what the fuck happened ? Jay lost his temper

He was on a bussiness trip when he got to know about the attack and he practically ran here to his brother He's still unconscious …we can't tell anything yet …the doctor informed scared of the most powerful families wrath Mr jahan patted jays shoulder to calm him down

Maya , Kabir's sister stood in corner crying when louis gave her coffee

She looked up n next she was in his arms …her home

…her peaceful place

Doctor came out with a tensed face …

Sir …he called father of Kabir , Jay and maya who along the guys stood up

He is conscious now …he informed making them all sigh

But …he hesitated making the men's tense

Due to the impact of accident he is temporarily paralysed His right arm along legs are paralysed

And here the doctor threw the bomb on them earning gasps from everywhere

Bakht was excited to visit the hospital tomorrow greeting
new patients was always able to boast her   She closed
her eyes sighing …here's to another
experience of her career

Chapter 2

Nervous huh? Amy nudged bakht in stomach making her about to fall

She regained her posture and glared at the girl who grinned showing her beautiful teeths

Amy took her to there boss ...yes she too is a doctor a orthopedic and work in same hospital

Amy barged in the office of her boss making him startle

Boss ...she is bakht and he is boss ...she noded satisfied smiling at her way of introducing them   Bakht wanted to punch her but let it be for home

She smiled polietly at mr micheal who seemed embarrassed

Welcome dr it's honor having you here he gave her a warming smile

And miss amy he turned to amy who was now sitting relax on his opposite chair like she own it

She look at bakht whoose eyes were out of her sockets

For the sake of icecream he's her fudging boss

So boss ...why u called me before the sun even rise ..amy exaggerate making micheal roll his eyes

She's too friendly !

Actually I need your consult for a case so we will proceed there he informed amy who frowned

Bakht will join us too .. I can't leave the poor girl alone in this whole wide world amy dramatically sighed making the other two scoff

Mr micheal gave bakht a small smile …umm yeah sure even a physiotherapist is required u can join us if u want? Sure … The girl agreed instantly it's better to be with amy than to bang her head on this huge hospital walls Amy clapped standing up making the chair fall with a thud

Oops …she bite her tongue but than jumped

Yeyyyy …we gonna rock she squeeled ..

For pastas sake amy..we are going to check a patient

Whatever …amy dismissed her animatedly

She's long lost sister of zoya …Bakht smiled at her thought

Zoya

How was she doing?

Is she married yet? Maybe

Let's go   …Amy's voice broke her trance and she followed the duo

Louis came out with jay from Kabir's room …

He is not taking the news as he should Jay sighed   Since Kabir got to know about his condition he is going mad and lashing on everyone

Malaika wiped her tears …my baby she cried making Zayn n Louis scoff

Overdramatic bitch Zayn mumbled under his breath

Guys I am gonna pray for my Kabir ….she announced and picked up her red bag to go out

She's praying in that party dress?Blake cringe making Zayn scoff

Yeah she's gonna pray at kitty parties …zayn replies sarcastically

Why do boss even tolerate her? Zayn sighed sitting on sofa

You know it don't u? …Blake too sat tired

Mr micheal's car stopped outside a huge mansion

Amy n bakht gasps …this is beautiful piece of brick

Shall we? Micheal's voice broke there trance and amy and bakht noded excited like a kids making the men chuckle

Bakht could feel her stomach doing summersault   She was having this feeling since she landed here but she avoided it

They entered the mansion and that moment three people froze

Zayn , Blake and bakht were face to face with each other

Tears filled bakhts eyes seeing her brother like partners all fit and grown up

Amy nudged her worried making her shake her head Ohh god where she landed herself?

Zayn n Blake didn't blink too shocked to react seeing there princess …there partner …there sister

Hello sir I am micheal n this is dr amy and Dr bakht we are here to check boss

On hearing that Bakht look at them confused Now who is boss here?

Blake snapped out and showed them the way but Zayn didn't left her sight making it difficult for her budge

Amy who saw this fumed …

She protectively stood before bakht and glared at Zayn Ohh hello mr …stop oggling okay? We know judo n I can kick ur ass she threatened making Zayn look at her Ohh boy she's beautiful …was the first thought that came in his mind

Chapter 3

Bakht cleared her throat averting her gaze from Zayn   It was extremely uncomfortable for her to be here at the first place but than she has to do it

Sighing she nudged amy who was shooting daggers at Zayn

Amy ..you … should go with dr micheal she meekly stated praying for amy to nod and go

Thankfully amy did nod and went where Blake took micheal leaving Zayn and Bakht alone

Hii …she shifts on her place intiating the convo while he stay rooted glaring her sandals

 Zayn?

No reply

Won't u talk?

No reply

Bakht bite her lip to stop the sob …her voice cracked

I.. understand …I just …she was about to turn when Zayn launched himself in her arms

U piece of plastic ….Zayn cried hugging her tightly making her tears spill out and she to hugged him back

I missed u donkey

I missed u princess both said together n laughed

Zayn wiped his nose in her stole making her shriek

Ewww..Bakht groaned

That's your punishment he evily grinned in return

Now .. now … Who is boss here? Bakht asked making

Zayn stiff

That …before he could say something mr micheal came

Hey … here come I will introduce you to boss he took bakht's hand in his n took her inside followed by a groaning Zayn

Boss can break his head for holding her hand …Zayn mumbled panicking

On reaching the room Bakht was met with Blake who averted his gaze

He's angry … And more he's hurt!

Her eyes landed on the figure on bed and the breath knock out of her system

Never in her wildest dream she imagined to meet her Kabir like this

She stumbled back eyes burning with tears

Blake n Zayn were quick to catch her n straighten her She caught there arms in death grip making the guys share knowing looks

He met with an accident and got partially paralysed micheal went on explaining

On hearing voices he opened his eyes and was met with bloodshot brown orbs

The eyes that looked straight in his soul …the eyes that had haunted him every night ..

There she stood …she has changed ..

She had got mature … a mature women …

Gone those bright color dresess now stood the women with elegent creame kurti with jeans

She is looking professional …but what caught his attention was her eyes …they have lost the twinkle in them …he can easily detect the dark circles under the layer of makeup

World still for both of them blurring everyone else

Dr are u there? Micheal shook Bakht by shoulder

Are u ok? He asked conserned making her nod

I…she trailed but they were intrupted by a shriek voice

Malaika jumped beside kabir on his bed n kissed his cheek

Aww baby look I came …she cling on him but his eyes were on her

Malaika looked up …ohh dr tell me when will my fiance be all ok?

 Fiance

Bakht looked at him shocked …he was already looking her and the shock n hurt on her face gave him peace

Umm …that Dr Bakht can tell micheal look at bakht Dr may we? He asked making bakht nod she had to be professional

Amy was done checking him its now her turn

She took confident steps towards him and start examining him

She touched his right leg n asked him in soft voice Does it hurt? While her eyes were fixed examining any other injury

I don't feel the pain anymore … His gruff voice came Her moments hault hearing his reply ….it was not a answer …it was a taunt …a cold taunt .

Gathering herself back she noded n scrubbed some jel and turned to dr micheal

Dr I guess his therapy has to wait till than these jels shall do

Micheal noded in adoration he loves people who are sincere with there profession

Thanku doctor .. it would be great if you visit him once before u return back dubai

This caught everyone's attention in the room and Bakht closed her eyes.

Chapter 4

Bakht looked around Zayn and Blake gave her disapproving glances while Kabir was just staring her expressionless

Amy who saw all this understood that something is wrong but what?

Bakht's phone rang making her startle

Hello

Where are u ? Wait! Are u dead ? Came shams voice

What do u want shams? Bakht whispered rolling her eyes

The guy informed her about him going out …least she scolds them for being careless

Bakht sighs looking at amy n mouthed shams making the girl nod

Umm …I think we should leave Bakht turned to dr micheal

Yeah sure …we have a dinner ahead micheal said to Bakht chuckling

Amy had bribed them that they will go for dinner tonight

On hearing this kabir clench his jaw …how dare he ask her out?

No …his voice was stern making everyone turn   I mean doc why not u join us for dinner he looked at micheal who too was confused

He looked Bakht n amy but Bakht spoke hurriedly in …umm dr micheal u can stay I …I need to leave she hurriedly said

No way she is having dinner with him and his fiance
. Amy understood that bakht is not comfortable n hurriedly
stood up
Let's go bakht …she holds bakht's hand and without
waiting for micheal the girls left the room   On
the way to the door Bakht bumps to someone
Oouch …. She winced rubbing her nose
Cupcake ?
C..cupc..ake? Fahad was flabbergasted seeing her in front
of him
Bakht looked at those warm eyes n couldn't resist n clung
to him hugging him to her life
He too had tears in his eyes …goshh …just how much he
missed this girl
His baby sister
Amy stood there smiling at the reunion she is no fool n
Hearing the name she had joined the dots   This
world is really small!
Zoya? Bakht whispered making Fahad sigh
Angry zoya was dangerous but pregnant and angry zoya
is scary …he made a face while Bakht was grinning   Ohh
my god she jumped excited … she squeeled at Fahad
making him laugh
I missed u bakht …he whispered making her gave him a
sad smile
Bakht …amy called her taking her back to reality
I need to go she took steps back making Fahad frown   But
..Fahad tried but bakht cut him off
Plzz … And tell zoya I have the name   she blinked
making Fahad smiled sadly

Zoya always wanted Bakht to name her child n vice varsa

Nodding she left with amy while Fahad stood watching her go

She was really here in bone n flash

Sighing he moved inside to check the after effects of storm that just passed

Amy and bakht entered the apartment and were met with silence

Bakht frowned .. arnt they gone yet?

Amy shrugged …

The girls moved to there rooms to freashen up but a earthshattering noise made them jump

Ohh my dog …shams clapped his hands on his mouth like a typical dramatic manner

Sahil avoided his dramatic squeel concentrating on his Nutella

She bloddy ditched him ….another feminine voice squeeled in shams ears making him fall from sofa   His coke was all over his face making amal burst in laughter

Bakht n amy barged in amal's room and the scene was like this

Shams was licking the coke from his face spread on floor

Amal was laughing like a lunatic

Sahil was eating Nutella while licking his fingers

Hii girls…amal jumped on

Shams's hand making him cry in pain

The girls groaned …

Now … When you guys have decided to be toddler let me be your strict mom .. bakht's voice was stern   Clean the room and yourself NOW!

Chapter 5

Hello mr mehmat …his gruff voice spoke

G…good m..Orni..ng boss it's my privellage to talk to u sir the owner of sunshine care was sluttering nervous and why not he's Talking to the Arabs the big boss   Hmm …u see Mr mehmat I need a physiotherapist for myself for like 2 months

Y..yes sir sure we will send the whole team ….but he cut him off sternly

Bakht shah…I want bakht shah only and with that the call was cut

Leaning on his headrest he closed his eyes reminiscing the all to familiar face

Welcome back carazon …he whispered with his famous smirk

Meanwhile others …

I am hungry like dogs .. I need FOOD

Amy glared her sister for screaming like a mad women but than again hungry amal is cranky

Guys … Eat as much as u want the bill is on me .. bakht smugly announced

Is she alright? Like what? Sahil gaped at her meanwhile shams did a happy dance   Free food .. good life!

They reached there table while Bakht excused herself to use powder room

Entering the lift she pulled her signature black leather jacket along her face mask ready to hunt

Reaching at room no.444 she knocked and the door was opened by an old men

The men frowned …yes?

Room service sir she said making him frown but he ignored it n moved at side talking on phone

Yeah that bastard got saved .. but how long I will make sure he ..

The men was talking in room when his door burst open followed by a kick on his head and next span his both hands were cut mercilessly making him cry in pain Kneeling down beside him Bakht smirked …dare you harm my men and I will rip ur head …her voice was dead calm making the men shudder

Goodby Ronaldo rest in hell with that he was stabbed multiple times in his stomach …right arm …and both legs Pulling out J she cleaned all the other evidences n flew out of room

This all happened in exact 11 mins and soon she was sitting with her friends like the old Bakht

This is her little secret … Well not little but yes! A secret They were chit chatting when a voice came making bakht jump

Holy fudge …zoya was standing with Fahad ,Zayn and Blake

Bakht turned back hugging her best friend her sister   U piece of plastic zoya screeched dramatically earning glares from people

Poor Fahad was busy apologizing with people for his wives indecent behaviour

After crying her heart out zoya digg in food ignoring everyone

Because hey …. Food is first love

Zayn moved aside eying amy with love puppy eyes

Blake looked away making bakht smile …tugging his sleeve she whispered

Won't you talk with your baby sister? …and here breaks his resolve she knew it that upon calling him brother he can forget even a murder

Pulling back from the hug he complaint cutely I am still angry

Bakht chuckled with teary eyes and sighed … Guess she has a lot of people to apologise to.

Chapter 6

Zoya lift sahil's chin examining him while his mouth was stuffed with chicken tikka

Baby .. what are u doing? Fahad tried to pull back her but she shushed him

Where's his jawline? Bakht has a sharp jawline and he doesn't seem like her brother…at all!

He is not from our family poor guy was adopted … Shams replied sipping his juice

Zoya noded agreeing with the information making Fahad frown

Zoya ….. Bakht took zoya's hand in hers making the girl smile softly

Zoya leaned n whispered in her ears making her stiff aren't you acting like we are talking after years ? chuckling zoya raised an eyebrow

Shutup zo … Bakht look at boys who were busy eating How did u even got to know about me ? Bakht asked making zoya grin

The girl shrugged .. nothing much . I just hijacked dad's office

Yes it was kabir's dad who helped her out of Russia n even he is the one behined the making of J Nodding Bakht hugged her best friend .

.I missed u zoo she chocked making zoya look at her

And next zoya was crying her eyes out startling everyone on table

And next hour was passed with all trying to calm the crying zoya

For the sake of ducks calm down …shams cried making zoya shut

How did u knew I love them?She wipe her tears n shams shrugg making zoya grin

Ok …she resumed eating making everyone gasp Shams … Did your mom ever went los Angeles ? Zayn couldn't help but ask

Huh .. than zoya's dad must have been to..before Zayn could complete he earned a smack

Owii … he glared Blake who rolled his eyes

With light laughters n chats the dinner passed happily

Bakht promised them all that she will meet them soon

4 days later ..

Dubai

But sir …Bakht tried to protest but her boss was admanent on sending her as Boss's physiotherapist

Sighing she noded knowing well that it has something to do with him

Ofcourse …her boss's body language is suspicious from the time she landed back in Dubai that is 2 days back Blake and Zayn had warned her that she will not cut them off now n she obliged fearing to loose them again   She called the number given by her boss in second ring the phone was lifted

Hello ..came his gruff voice making her shiver

I will not come alone …I have responsibility of my brother's if u want me as your physiotherapist   my brother's will come along … She said in a stern voice trying hard not to slutter

A deep sigh was heard …ok! and the call was cut

Shams n sahil were more than excited listning the news

We arnt going on vaccations …Bakht groaned making the boys shrugg

Meanwhile in Doha

He was killed mercilessly …louis said looking at the picture they got

Irony is .. on the same day we were there in the same hotel in excitement Zayn blurted

And what were u guys doing there? Kabir raised an eyebrow

Blake facepalms himself while Fahad glared the guy   We went there to eat duh ..zoya entered n answered saving the boys

Yes boss! Sister-in-law wanted to eat the table .. no! I mean the food … Zayn grinned like a an idiot   Kabir curtly noded dismissing them…he's not stupid he knows by the broad smiles that they were with her

Closing his eyes he leaned on headrest …he want to hurt her that's why he had called her here to make her suffer But the bigger question here is will he be able to do this? And the other question hunting him is who is this J Bcz clearly this person is protecting him n his family

…but why?

 Only tym can tell ….

Past

Chapter 7

It all started 5 years back when one fateful trip brought bakht shah back to her lost best friend

She was happy with her life … A normal life with her aunt rosy

After the death of her mom aunt rosy who was also bestfriend of her mom took care of her

Bakht never saw her mom … She was one when she passed away leaving her alone in this world   Her dad took care of her with the help of Aunt rosy   But there were more people who loved bakht to pieces

Mr Jahan and his family .. where his eldest son jay loved her as his sister maya was her bestie meanwhile Kabir Her best friend .. her first crush … And .. her first boyfriend

The friendship turned into innocent liking and growing up Kabir was more protective over bakht

With time the protectiveness changed into posessiveness and when they turned 17 they confessed there love   It was her birthday she had just turned 18 and they celebrated it along one year of togetherness

Bakht couldn't be more happier having such loving people around her

Until

Until the next day of her birthday 16th June she woke up with a smile and went down to greet her father good morning

But bakht didn't knew that nothing was same … Her father greeted her back and after getting ready she rushed out to his house   But it was locked

Running back home she was informed by rosy aunt that the Jahan's had left

Left? How can he leave her? Just like that?

She called him for days .. texted him .. visited his locked house daily but got no reply and when bakht turned 20 she knew that he's never gonna be back

So she too decided to move on and from that time she never took his name nor she visited his house that was once there's

In these years she drifted apart from her dad because he made himself distinct .. the only family she had was aunt rosy and zoya

Her soul sister .. her best friend

They met on the first day of college when bakht was searching for her department and zoya was probably ragging her seniors

The girls clicked immediately with bakht's wittiness and zoya's boldness they made the sassy duo

And now here she is in last year of her degree … She will become physiotherapist and she couldn't be more happier

Russia

Zo .. can u wakeup already? We are here for internship Bakht groaned nudging her best friend who was sleeping with no worries

Wakeup or else I am going alone .. she yelled in her ears

Stop screaming women my ears will start bleeding …
Zoya sat up huffing

Let's go .. I am so excited … Bakht jumped in excitement while zoya rolled her eyes

Who the fudge gets excited to visit hospitals?

The girls reached the hospital but the whole hospital was dead silent

Are we at wrong adress? Wait I think we are in a morgue?

Shutup zee! Bakht took steps towards the room

Dr Tuber? She opened the door but the sight that welcomed her made her gasp   What the fruit cake?

Chapter 8

———◆———

B…bakht? Zoya whispered to her friend who was frozen on the sight of four men sitting in front of the dead doctor leisurely

All four eyes snapped at the girls direction

 Ohh hoo!

Her hazel eyes clashed with the steely grey ones making her shudder

Bakht RUN .. zoya whispered yelled making her jump

The girls turned and ran as fast as they can but the gunshots were heard in the corridor

She lost her balance tripping over her feets and landed on the floor with a thud

Zoya cursed her helping her to stand when they were surrounded by three unknown faces

We don't have to kill the pretty girls .. one of them said more like whinned

Zayn .. the other one growled pointing gun at zoya's head who huffed

Bakht hissed trying to stand up as her twisted ankel was now swollen

She again stumbled when the guy with brown curly hairs stepped to give her his hand

 Arnt u here to kill us? She frown

You want to die? He raised an eyebrow while zoya hissed near her

Shutup don't provoke him you stupid

DON'T FUCKING TOUCH HER

Bakht froze hearing the voice … She was yet again met with the grey eyes that now seemed familiar   Her head started spinning and last she recalled was loosing her balance

I got you carazon … Was the soft whisper that echoed in her ear before she lost her consciousness

Next she woke up with a heavy head and bandaged ankle in a five-star hotel room

Wait … What?

She looked around and spotted zoya pacing in front of her bed

The girl nearly squelled seeing her ….. good god u scared the living days out of me ..

Where are we? Her bestfriend glared her

Ohh .. we were on vaccations in a hospital where we witnessed a murder than your highness decided to trip and fall and than faint and now we are captives of those big men's … Zoya took a deep breath after narrating everything that too very sarcastically

Zoya .. we need to leave .. bakht panicked remembering the icy grey eyed men

Yeah .. I have called our cart we will be leaving after lunch are u HOBO ??

We are KIDNAPPED , freaking KIDNAPPED

Bakht tried calming her best friend who had probably lost her shits

But who is she kidding she is shuddering with the fact that she is his captive

Uh .. zoya I need to tell you something

Don't tell me you fall in love with one of them

Shutup .. she glared at her best friend

You know the guy with grey eyes? She bite her lip

Yeah who growled don't touch her like dude I nearly died there .. zoya rolled her eyes

He's Kabir

Whatever I … WHAT??

Zoya was now gaping like a fish while bakht felt her eyes welling up with tears

Why have we kidnapped them? Fahad frown at his bestfriend who was in deep thoughts

Yeah .. boss the girls witnessed the murder they can be harmful .. Blake too looked at his boss in confusion

It's rule in mafia .. one mistake can cause several lives …

It's her Fahad … A broken whisper echoed   It's my carazon(heart).

Chapter 9

Ohh my crushed potatoes!

Are you freaking serious? I mean wohooo … Bakht hushed zoya who was squeeling like a kid

Zee stop screaming we arnt in a amusement park .. bakht gritted making her best friend scowl

It's not my fault ok? We are kidnapped by 4 hotshot mafia guys n one of them is your ex how can I not FREAK OUT She shouted the last part making bakht cringe

Soon the door was opened by Zayn who grinned at the girls waving a hey

Uh hi? Bakht was unsure making zoya snicker

Hey .. zoya yelled enthusiastically making Zayn grin wider

Let's go .. everyone is waiting …. The girls looked at each other afraid

Zayn seemed to sense there pale faces n chuckle .. for dinner he added making the girl visibly relax

They reached the table where Kabir sat with Blake , louis n Fahad his trusted men and friends

Zayn was youngest among all and the mischievous one too

The girls however refused to sit and eat making guys grunt

Why have you guys kidnapped us? Are u some sort of thieves … Look we don't have money ! Zoya exclaimed horrified the guys gave her a bored look

Bakht could feel an intense gaze on her but she refused to acknowledge it

Have your food n stop screaming in my ears … Fahad grunted looking at the girl who narrowed her eyes

Are u kidding me? Are u hobos? We are dying here because u idiots kidnapped us and u want me to eat?? She yelled again

Louis griited out taking out his pistol making bakht gasp in horror

Z..zee she held her best friend's hand who seemed to be way furious to get scared

Uh .. you can't kill us wait! Go ahead kill me … I promise I will haunt you wearing white gown and white hairs n yeah those long scary nails till your death

My soul will be here scaring the day lights out of you YOU BUNSHEES she screamed

She took a deep breath after her speech looking at everyone bakht looked ready to faint while Kabir was busy staring her

Louis and Blake looked at her gaping like a fish .. Zayn saluted her grinning while Fahad had an amused look

Fahad take miss zoya with you and give her some juice she must be tired of screaming .. Kabir finally spoke making zoya huff

Bakht held her best friend's hand protectively glaring at Kabir

Don't you dare come near us .. she warned him standing in front of zoya who scowled

I won't harm you carazon .. he spoke slightly hurt   You cannot harm me Kabir jahan .. you already have done enough .. she icily spoke making him clench his jaw   Uh bakht? Zoya tried stopping her emotional best friend

Why are you not killing us already? That's what you do right? Kill people and enjoy! That's your work … Comeon go ahead finish me Kabir jahan and get done with it

Zoya wanted to clap and cry at the same time finally her innocent bakhtii is speaking for herself like yayy!   While she was busy grinning she was dragged away by a scaring looking Fahad   Hey don't drag me you idiot I am not a suitcase …. She yelled making him smile

Who the heck are you girl? He shake his head slightly chuckling

Zoya realised that bakht is alone down there and cursed herself

Ohh huh …!

Chapter 10

————◆————

Kabir looked at the girl he loved soo much she looked broken

He took a step closer making her flinch and step away

He didn't liked it ... A bit!

Carazon

Don't call me that .. I am not yours anymore Kabir jahan .. her sentence infratuated him more

In a swift motion he yanked her towards himself making her gasp

You were born to be mine bakht .. you always were mine .. my carazon .. he carrased her cheeks

Leave me .. she wriggled out of his hold flustered with the proximity

I had to leave bakht .. it was necessary we cannot risk the lives of people living there .. our lives were in threat .. she looked at him with a frown

Dad was a mafia he always was .. we knew it me and Jay were trained to be mafia ... Bakht gasp at this   The sweet uncle was freaking mafia!

Maya and you were unknown to it because we wanted you to be mature enough to understand ... She glared at him on being called immature making him bite back his smile His carazon is cutest!

That night dad was being informed about the threat and we flied here and after that we were being attacked by rivals

It took years for things to get back to normal after the chaos dad contacted uncle who informed that you moved out

She looked at him grasping the information but a frown etched her face

But dad never told me .. her dad never spoke about Jahan's

Maybe you never asked .. he smiled sadly making her feel guilty all of a sudden

You know … He whispered standing close to her   I came the night we were leaving .. her eyes widen did he came to meet her?

Yeah .. n you were dead asleep like a log! She scoffed but agreed with her subconscious

He carrased her cheeks .. I have been searching you for so long my love and finally I got you .. he smiled with glee Maya would be so happy to see you and Jay he would probably … Bakht pulled back making him frown   I..I can't n..no! She sluttered making Kabir look at her confused

What are u saying carazon?

Kabir .. this … We it's not gonna work ..shaking her head she took a sharp breath

I am a normal girl with normal life I do not wish to be a part of this blood war I can't … Her voice cracked at the end making his heart shattered

I fucking love you dammit! He yelled loosing his calm But I don't … Look! It was past .. I have moved on its better to .. she was cut off when he chuckled darkly Bakht shah I fucking love you from the second I met   you …

you want me to forget that? You want me to fucking leave you ? After all these years ... No my love you are wrong! Bakht shuddered looking at his cold face n instinctively took steps back scared of him

Clenching his jaw he harshly tugged her towards him either you love me yourself or I will make you love me he whispered in her ears n bakht knew the moment that She's doomed!

Chapter 11

You are insane … She pushed him away with tears leaking her eyes

I am not a doll Kabir .. you cannot just switch off and on my feelings … She screamed at him

You left me

You lied

You returned and now it's YOU who want me back Where am I? Where's bakht? It was always what Kabir wanted … You never cared what I think … Just leave me Kabir I don't want to see you Go! Just Go! She started crying hysterically making him panick

Okay bakht hey relax … He panicked seeing her breathing heavily

Fuck! Bakht breath baby where the fuck is doctor?

LOUIS

BLAKE

He yelled for his men's seeing her loosing her conscious He carried her in his arms carrying her to his room in sheer fear

What if he looses her again? No! He fucking can't   What did you did to her you pig! Zoya ran towards her bestfriend

Fudge! She had another attack .. she mumbled

What? Kabir looked at her confused

Hello mr curly hairs she waved at Fahad … Take your friend out I need to treat her

No! I won't leave her .. Kabir immediately refused making zoya glare him

Do u wish to be thrown from this balcony? She raised an eyebrow and for a moment the guys looked at her flabbergasted

Zoya felt flushed feeling there gazes and cleared her throat .. I need to loose her shirt now GO she semi-yelled In another minute the room was empty and they were given all the privacy   Idiots

She scoffed loosing bakht's shirt turning her over she rubbed her back the thing she knows will help   She knew bakht and was well aware that she gets panick attacks but the idiot mafia didn't

Ohh how she wish to stab them all with her shinny metal fork!

You must have messed the shit up .. Jay barged in his study making him roll his eyes

She had a panick attack and I think she often gets them .. Kabir looked thoughtful

I can't believe cupcake is here .. Jay smiled softly   She hates me .. probably us! Kabir sighed

She's right on her place … Give her some time k .. Jay advised his brother

How can I stay away from her brother? I fucking want her with me to keep me sane he slammed his punch on the wall

Zoya narrowed her eyes at maya who shifted uncomfortably

After bakht regained consciousness maya barged in the room and after crying for straight 20 mins both bakht and maya told zoya everything

When the guys tried entering the room maya threw her brother's out stating it's girls time

Zoya stop scaring her .. bakht rolled her eyes smiling at maya who sighed seeing zoya grin

She suddenly Clapped her hands jumping on bed .. just when I thought my life is boring we witnessed a murder got kidnapped and now stuck with my best friend's ex and his family

Fun-freaking-tastic !

She threw her hands in air dramatically making maya laugh while bakht scoffed

Her bestfriend is a drama queen.

Chapter 12

A week passed like this with girls ignoring boys like they ignore there growing nails

Kabir had enough he needed to talk to her he knew she's angry at him and but she needs to know she can't leave him again

He won't let her go now .. his study door was knocked and soon a grinning Maya barged in

I didn't tell you to come in … His sister rolled her eyes at his rude remark

I am taking the girls on shopping .. she announced

What? Why? He stood up immediately on her mention

You freaking kidnapped them and they don't have clothes here .. till when are u planning on them borrowing my stuffs … She glared at her brother who rubbed his neck sheeplessly

Uh yeah .. take Fahad and Zayn with you

Maya shrugged muttering a cool when Kabir called her   I am not breaking the sister code bro sorry .. the girl apologetically smiled at him making him groan

Mr curly hairs … Here zoya shoved another bag in fahad's face making the guy groan

Zayn laughed along maya at his state .. zoya was the first one who was dictating the rude , strict Fahad

After shopping to there hearts content the girls decided to eat something

Bakht smiled looking at the banters of zoya and Zayn over food

Last one week she thought a lot about him n the entire situation

Idly … It's the circumstances that were wrong both of them are right on there places .. she wanted to give him a chance because at the end the truth remains same that is she still loves him

She decided that she's going to talk and clear all the things with kabir

She was eating her pizza enjoying the compony when suddenly the area was echoing with gunshots   Fahad and Zayn immediately covered the girls shooting

Maya too took out her gun making bakht and zoya gasp

What the actual DUCK? Zoya whisper yelled

Fahad was shot in his arm making girls squeel .. bakht rushed to him but she was yanked away from her group by a masked men

Wriggling she tried to push the men off her when the guy was shot straight on his head by Zayn

you okay? She noded too scared to speak

They somehow managed the whole scenario and returned home

Kabir was shaking in rage his jaw was clenched while eyes were red .. bakht couldn't recognise the guy which made her gulp the lump

This isn't her Kabir …

He held her hand his gaze set on the red marks on her wrist

How fucking dare he touch her? He growled at his men's

K..Kabir calm down .. she held his arm who was raging in anger

Boss .. they know about bakht .. Zayn informed him making him curse loud

There will be two gaurds with her always … Double the security and maya start training them he barked the orders Bakht looked at them dumbfolded .. this isn't what she wanted .. this isn't her place.

Chapter 13

Kabir could feel her getting distant

She always had fear in her eyes and was hesitant while talking with him

After that day maya had started training her and zoya

She had started talking with him but that wasn't her   His carazon was carefree not afraid , she was fierce not meek and he blamed himself for her change

No matter how much I try I mess things up .. why my life is so fucked up? He smashed the glass on wall   What did the poor glass did to you? Louis scowled at him You need to give her time k .. she needs space to set her mind

Brother .. will she leave me ?   Kabir looked like a vulnerable kid at that moment and Jay hated seeing him like that

No! She won't … Get a grip men you are Kabir jahan you don't fear anything

I fear her being away Jay .. Kabir slumped on his chair

Bro stop being a love sick we are fucking mafias we don't beg we snatch what is ours … Fahad spoke hissing at his best friend

Right! I agree with him .. give her some time she won't be able to run anyway .. Blake shrugged

Kabir heaved a cold sigh …

Why are you sulking here? I mean you sulk everywhere but why here? Zoya sat beside her bestfriend

Zee .. we cannot live here this isn't our world .. bakht gave her a perplexed look

Zoya sighed shaking her head .. no bakht this is where you belong

To him

Bakht looked at her shocked while zoya smiled   I have seen the way he looks at you like you are the most precious to him .. he loves you bakhtii give him a chance .. zoya squeezed her hand gently

Besides I think I like mr curly hair .. like he's so wild the girl smirked making bakht gasp at her words   The best friends laughed enjoying there time together

Bakht really thanked her lord for blessing her with zoya … She's her sunshine

She knocked on his study door mentally kicking herself and zoya

Her gaurds stood beside her with a poker face

Arnt you guys hungry? She frowned at them   No mam .. came the robotic reply making her huff in annoyance

Why do u not look in my eyes? Am I that bad? She pouted

You are too good for them to look …. His deep voice made her jump

You startled me .. she whispered making him smile

Come .. he held her hand taking her inside

You still are obsessed with black .. she shook her head looking at his interior that was all black   He grinned leaning on his desk   I don't forget the things I love carazon .. she looked away feeling herself blushing at that

Okay bakht get a grip! Her subconscious scolded Clearing her throat she spoke I need my phone and other things from my hotel

Why?

Are u serious?

I was always serious about you

Can you stop! She blushed yet again while he smirked But seriously … I need my things I need to contact aunt she explained making him nod

It will be with you tomorrow … Anything else?

Well … She looked here and there

Thankyou

Thankyou? He frowned

Yeah .. u know for protecting us from those mens that day Kabir took steps near her .. noone can harm a hair on your head carazon I won't let them .. he held her hand posessively

I know you won't … Words stumble out of her mouth leaving both stunned .

Chapter 14

Mr Jahan was happily surprised finding bakht in his house What a great surprise you brothers have given me .. he exclaimed happily kissing bakht's forhead lovingly   Dad you need give the credit to that doctor because of him

Kabir found her … Jay grinned

Suddenly bakht and zoya gasp looking at guys who smiled sheeplessly

Uh …. We can explain …. Fahad nervously looked at zoya who crossed her arms over her chest

You better before I smash your head like crushed potatoes .. she blew the imaginary dust from her hands dramatically

Uh .. he wasn't a doctor .. he was doing illegal bussiness under the tag of doctor

As if you guys sell milk , that too with loyalty .. zoya sarcastically smiled

He was involved in human trafficking .. Kabir gritted making the girl gasp

And we were about to do internship under that pig … Zoya screeched horrified with the idea

I like this young women .. she is witty .. Mr Jahan laughed making zoya grin while others just shake there head Indeed is she wittiest!

Uh .. uncle Can you tell me why father never talked about you after you left ? Is he .. bakht hesitated to ask about her father

Child! He cares for you he loves you a lot it's just he's …
He was protecting you .. he had lost your mom once he didn't want to loose you

Bakht closed her eyes .. it means he is also involved with you guys?

No my child he is a honest loyal men who hates violence Mr jahan shake his head remembering his friend

 he distanced himself from me the day you guys left .. I was left all alone uncle she sniffed

My child! Mr Jahan hugged her she was always like a daughter to him and seeing her cry ached his heart

I am sorry sweety u had to bear all the pain alone .. but now you are here with us .. everything will be fine .. he assured her

Soon the girls started talking distracting bakht while gents were busy in discussing bussiness

It was just another day when bakht was trying to wake zoya up who wasn't planning on coming out of the bed

God women go away I am sleepy .. zoya mumbled in her pillow

I won't it's afternoon zee comeon …Cried ger bestfriend

Bakht go … Eat Kabir's head leave me with my pillow we are busy shoo .. zoya yelled now snuggled up in her blanket

I won't talk to you .. pouting bakht stomped her feet getting out of her room huffing

Owii .. she bumped in Kabir who looked at her amused

Why are u all red my Love? He teased her earning himself a glare

Zoya isn't waking up .. maya isn't home and guys are busy somewhere she made a face

That's so heartbreaking he feigned sadness making her scowl

I am angry right now don't provoke me more I can punch you ok? She showed him her tiny punch making Kabir laugh at her cuteness

Oh carazon you are the cutest .. he cooed her but than sobered up looking at her irritated face

Okay let's go … He dragged her with him to there adventure.

Chapter 15

No freaking way!

Bakht gasp looking at the stable of horses

I am not riding them … She shake her head violently making Kabir chuckle

Right you arnt riding them alone .. we will be riding them .. he grinned but she felt like hiding herself in her room Kabir you know I hate horses you can't do this … She took a step back while he smirked muschiviously That's the fun mi carazon (my heart) he evily laughed while she made a run to save herself with him after her Both laughed to there hearts content running behind each other, teasing each other just like old times

Okay … He panted stopping making her stuck her tongue at him

You are such a kid .. he shake his head sitting near the stables

Says who? She raised an eyebrow making him smile   I missed you bakht .. this smile … The giggles .. I missed everything about you … I missed us .. he held her hand making her heart flutter

I missed you too Kabir .. you never really left you were always in my head no matter where I went you were there

… He grinned innocently

  Can u give us a chance bakht?

I am trying Kabir … Give me sometime

I can wait for you my whole life my love .. just remember one thing he joined there forheads

I need you to survive .. he breathed in her scent making her shiver with tingles

Later that day the girls were in living room with boys playing vedio games

It seemed like a happy family spending time together just like normal people do

They were pretty normal except for the fact that the girls were being kidnapped by the guys who turned out to be mafias

As normal as that!

Can u believe it! I mean how fudging good I played .. zoya squeeled

Yeah now stop jumping on the sofa you arnt a monkey .. Fahad chided her

Mr curly hair do you want to be bald? She asked with a poker face making Zayn and Blake snickered beside her

Zee .. bakht gasp at her bestfriend who was hell bent on irritating Fahad

He won't do anything to her that bastard is whipped … Blake smirked at his friend

Fahad just sat there with a straight face but zoya could see the twitch of his lips for a second

And that was enough for her to keep doing what she's been on

Bakht dialled her aunt and bite her lip in anxiousness The phone was picked up on second ring

Aunt .. how are you? I was so worried u weren't replying to my texts

Bakht .. my child .. she frown finding her aunt crying

What's the matter aunt? Are u alright?

I am ok child but your dad .. bakht felt her breath hitch

W…what happened? She held the recliner of her bed tightly

He's been shot yesterday and he can't survive .. phone fell from her hand and tears welled up her eyes numbing her senses

Her father is killed!

Chapter 16

Bakht look at the clear sky holding back another sob   Her whole body trembled crying the whole night in pain and guilt

Pain of loosing her father .. guilt to not be there when she was needed for him

Aunt rosy had declined her to come back as it's dangerous for her because seems those people were after her   Kabir entered her room and his heart clenched seeing her crying

He knew it .. ofcourse he's a mafia afterall .. he wanted to tell her in the morning but seems she got to know somehow

Bakht my love … She looked at him teary eyed and next a heart-wrenching sob escaped her lips

He immediately engulfed her in a hug while she hide herself in his chest shaking with sobs   He let her cry and mourn over her father … She felt asleep in his arms while he held her closer

Her tear stricken face pained him but he knew that no words can comfort when a close one is snatched away He promised himself to kill those people in the most brutual ways to revenge his uncle's death

Clenching his jaw he tug her to bed and decided to stay back if she wakes up again she will need him   Bakht opened her eyes feeling a arm around her waist looking down she looked at kabir's sleeping figure

He was in a uncomfortable position sitting while his head snuggled in her stomach while arm drapped around her protectively

She remembered how he consoled her with his silence and how he provided her comfort with his embrace

Stroking his hairs her eyes welled up .. those people are after her she knows .. what if they do something to his family or him?

She would die just from the mere thought .. kissing his forehead she admired him

The men she loved since she gained senses .. her first friend .. crush .. love he is everything

You are too precious to loose Kabir .. she mumbled

You say I am your heart your carazon she smiled carrasing his subtle cheeks I have always carried your heart with me , within me

With one last kiss she stood up adjusting blanket on him

Kabir wokeup with a aching neck he looked around and upon not finding her panick rose in him

Good morning .. her soft voice relaxed him

Good morning love .. his husky voice made her smile

He observed her who was now setting breakfast for them

Fidgiting with her fingers she nervously glance at him

Umm .. breakfast?

He held her hand making her sit on the sofa

Bakht my heart .. are u ok ? She blinked at him

I am trying to be okay Kabir … And with you by my side I will succeed .. he grins at that nodding

Let's do the breakfast than .. he changed the topic trying to distract her

She smiled and the duo did there breakfast with him fussing over how much less she eats and how much she has became weak

I am healthy and I eat healthy .. she pouted but he only rolled his eyes filling her plate with fruits making her whin .

Chapter 17

Kabir had instructed everyone to act normal around bakht
He knows how much she gets uncomfortable with sympathy and attention
Boss they are the same people who killed our men's back in Australia
He clenched his jaw .. we are Russian mafias and they can't do shit here
But we need to be extra careful because now they are after bakht and you know the guy is fucking psycho .. Jay clenched his fist
I won't let him have a glimpse of her .. Kabir gritted
Next hour went by with them barking orders on everyone
Mr Jahan had came to meet bakht and was spending time with girls
The guys tried looking as normal as they can but the red bloodshot eyes were evident of the sleepless night   Did you all were on hunt ? Are u guys vampires? Zoya dramatically gasp looking at Fahad
Can you for a minute not utter nonsense? Louis gritted
Aye captain .. I will kick you in your butt if you say something to my daughter's .. mr Jahan smacked the guys head making him wince
Fahad raise an eyebrow at zoya who smugly hugged mr Jahan
Daughter eh?

She scrunched her nose in annoyance .. do you want to see the adoption paper? He scowled hearing her witty comeback while others laugh

Are you alright? Bakht looked at him conserned Yes my love .. he smiled a tired one making her narrow her eyes at him

No Kabir you arnt come .. she commanded and the ruthless mafia boss meekly obliged following her order

Others suppressed there smiles looking at her bossing around there boss while Zayn and Blake were thankful to there partner finally boss is going to sleep which means they can also sleep in peace

Ohh my white pillows I am coming .. Zayn dramatically cried running to his room

Mr curly hair you should sleep or you will start looking like an own and I certainly not wish to be associated with one .. zoya gasp at the end making Fahad shake his head

Remind me why I even tolerate you?

Duh because you love me

Miss zoya .. he turned to her shocked who herself was frozen

Uh .. no delete that from your memory pretend it never happened or else I will kill u … now Go! She yelled at last hiding her red face

Fahad just laughed highly amused by the beauty

She surely has no filter not that he's complaining I am getting so cozy vibes like wow .. boss is no more in a mad mood with a frown instead he smiles all because of my darling bakht .. Zayn cooed her who gave him a funny look

Huh? U see our sulking king also knows as mr curly here had also left his usual scowl instead he had expression on his face .. Blake boasted

Yeah .. shocked and stunned are the most popular ones .. Zayn snickered looking at zoya who threw her chips packet on him

He didn't bothered to return it instead he ate it all happily much to zoya's annoyance

Let's cook something bakhti I am craving your handmade pasta

Okay … But you won't try to cook .. bakht sternly ordered Why? The girl whinned

Because dear zoya we can't burn this kitchen as well This shuts zoya up who mumbles a fudge off leaving behind laughing Zayn and Blake .

Chapter 18

The days passed with no suspicious activity and everyone was now getting used to the routine

Specially bakht with four gaurds around her and Zayn always joint to her hip

Don't take her wrong she loves the guy as her brother but the brat is most annoying and irritating at times like right now

Arnt you my sister? Will not you help your poor handsome brother? Is this it .. was it the end of your love? The guy dramatically cried

I am not asking Kabir to let you buy a sports bike when you clearly are clumsy as zoya .. zoya who was smiling at something hearing her bestfriend scowl

I am not ... She stood up in defence but tripped and almost fell on floor proving bakht right

Fine .. she huffed glaring at her bestfriend who smugly noded

Kabir is rubbing on her .. look at that evil smirk .. Zayn whispered to zoya who noded

Yeah .. my bestfriend was sweet , innocent and naïve what have your boss done to her .. my poor bakhtii she cried

Will you guys stop bitching about Kabir and help me instead? Bakht asked them irritated

Uh .. are u like pregnant ? Zayn grin nervously   What the DUCK?

What the fuck?

Two voices echoed .. bakht was gaping like a fish while

Kabir was rooted on his place

Okay .. I was just joaking because she's having severe mood swings Zayn held his hands up in surrender Bakht than narrowed her eyes at Kabir trying to intimidate him

What did you just said? The guy looked at her nervously

What baby? He tried feigning innocence

No cursing in this house Kabir jahan or I will kick you out understood? At this moment Kabir looked like a kid who was getting scolded by his mom

What a relief to my ears .. Blake cried looking at his boss getting scolded

She's on her periods guys .. just stay away she gets scary .. zoya shuddered making guys gulp

OHKAY .. the guys mentally noted to not be in bakht's bad reach

What's happening? Jay grinned entering the kitchen where the gang was hanging out nowadays   Courtesy to bakht and her baking!

Uh .. nothing we were discussing how bakht gets all macho and literally kicked boss out for cursing … Blake seriously passed the information making Jay Chuckle Ohh that's good .. that bastard needs to tone down that Jay shrugged nonchalantly

Mr Jahan had decided to dine in with them with Jay and maya as the trio do not live in the mansion

How's your training going on my princesses? Mr Jahan beamed at zoya and bakht

Ohh it's going like butter on bread …. Except for the fact that we need to get our ass up at 4am run 6kms than practice with maya like mad for 3 hrs straight it's going absolutely fantastic , stunning …. Zoya passed a tight lipped smile

Uh dad .. bakht glared her bestfriend .. what she means is it's going good .. the men laughed it off shaking his head at zoya's dramatics

Boss

One of the men came making the guys alert   What? Louis stood up alarmed

There's a guy saying he knows where to find laila   All of them froze on the name and bakht and zoya looked confused .

Chapter 19

———◆———

Laila is Blake's twin sister

W…what? Bakht sat shocked

After the morning incident the guys had rushed out of the house leaving girls with Zayn

And now maya sat cross legged along Zayn telking them about laila

Yeah .. he was 17 when he and his sister were separated .. she was being sold

S..sold? Zoya gasp while bakht sat there shocked   Yeah .. that's what Blake remembers they were being kidnapped and his sister was sold while he was tied

They took her away from him and he couldn't do anything heck he was himself sedated … Zayn gritted

That's why he joined us .. brother trained him and from years he's searching for his sister … Maya concluded Bakht felt her eyes stinging .. the guy who's always smiling is hiding so much of pain within him   They heard footsteps and immediately rushed down to see that Kabir was back along Louis and fahad

Where's he? Maya whispered looking at her brother   He wanted to be alone . Fahad spoke

Bakht went to him who hasn't came out if his study the time he had returned

What Blake did was so courageous .. Jay's voice hault her Yeah choosing someone else above own blood is so difficult

He says she's his sister … Her heart dropped at that Blake calls her his sister … Did he ?

Ohh god!

He chose bakht over laila and I will make sure I bring laila to him .. his voice was rough

We will find laila even for that I had to give my life … Kabir spoke

We will brother .. Blake is our mate .. Jay noded   While she retreated her steps back to save her Blake had to sacrifice his sister

Tears welled up her eyes … What of tomorrow they ask Kabir to give up everything because of her?   He will in a blink of an eye … Her inner voice spoke   No .. he can't .. I can't risk so many lives I can't … She whispered wiping her tears   She sat there all night in the cold that didn't effect her but she needed to clear her mind   Zoya?

Zoya looked at her bestfriend horrified

What bite your face? It's so swollen? She screeched

It's nothing … Bakht waved it off

Zee can you promise me one thing .. at this her bestfriend raised an eyebrow

If someday I won't be with you will you forgive me?

What even .. bakht hushed her

Promise me zee .. please .. she pleaded

Fine no need to cry jeez! I will but why are u saying like that .. zoya had a frown

Nothing just feeling emotional .. bakht wiped away her tears hugging her bestfriend

Also , do marry Fahad he's a nice guy and probably the only one who can tolerate you .. she chuckled feeling her bestfriend scowl

Whatever .. now don't scare me bakhtii u arnt going anywhere away from me and if u are planning to run away let's do it together .. she wriggled her eyebrows   Who's running away? Both groan hearing Kabir who was now glaring at them

I swear if you guys even think … Zoya rolled her eyes Bakht ask him to calm his donkeys I am not taking you away from your Romeo … Bakht smacked her arm looking at Kabir who was looking at her in suspicion

It's nothing Kabir .. we were joaking around   You better be carazon because I won't mind killing anyone who take u away from me   She gulped nodding meekly.

Chapter 20

We will be back till tomorrow you guys will stay inside the house

Girls do not even go in lawn … All of us will not be here and leaving you with gaurds is not so satisfying …

Fahad spoke

Chill bro .. I am here and I won't let them jump around maya assured her brother's

What are you mother hen? Zoya frowns at her

Bakht

Yes Kabir

Please stay safe for me , will you?

She looked at his handsome face as if memorising it

I will

And Kabir .. be back safe without any scratch

He smiled kissing her head .. I will carazon .. I will

You will get her back brother my prayers are with you guys .. bakht hugged Blake who noded with a small smile

The guys left for antartica where Noah was hiding with laila as sources informed

How about I cook today? Bakht suggested making both zoya and maya grin widely

Sure go ahead infact bake a cake as well I am craving it since I was born

Maya giggled on the silly joak while bakht gave a bored look to her best friend   That was lame

I am your bestfriend you have to laugh it's in our agreement .. the women cried dramatically

Maya take care of this kid .. bakht pointed at zoya who pouted

She prepared food for them and the girls decided to binge watch movies to kill time

The girls ate with chit chats and after sometime bakht saw her besties getting asleep while she sighed coldly

Maya and zoya woke up with groans and heavy heads They found furious looking Kabir and fahad pacing here and there

Where's bakht? Maya was the one to get up first

Louis handed her a note his face tensed

Dear friends ,

I know you guys will be furious on me but know that I am doing it for good . I have to leave or else you guys will be in danger .

But I assure you .. I will be safe and protected . Do not worry about me and please don't search me .   Ps. Sorry zee and maya I kind of sedated you and gaurds as well

She can't leave me alone .. zoya got up her voice shaking She left

Two words and Kabir felt like the biggest looser

She left him alone

He lost her   Again

She didn't even think how will he live without her?   He fucking need her to breathe .. he smashed the bottle on wall screaming in agiation   We

need to search her .. Jay spoke

No!

Everyone looked at Kabir shocked who had a emotionless face

Noone will go after her .. she wanted to leave .. she left
Noone is going to search her .. let her be where she feels safe
Maybe this was there end .. maybe Kabir and bakht weren't meant to be …

Present

Chapter 21

Bakht took a sharp breath standing outside his mansion
The large oak doors were opened and she was met with
all to familiar dark brown orbs
Mr jahan smiled softly at his little warrior
Dumping her bags she hugged the old men snuggling in
his warmth

My champion ...he whispered making her smile
Holding her by shoulders he kissed her head ...welcome
back doll this made bakht eyes moist
Shams n sahil were standing there with there mouth hung
open
Ohh my dog! What a piece of oak ...shams exclaimed
Bakht introduced them to Mr jahan ...patting the young
men the old men noticed scars on his neck n his eyes raged
Bakht blinked assuring him making him calm   Come
...he took them inside ...it was early morning so noone
was up yet
He showed shams sahil there room n took Bakht to hers
The room was beside Kabir's room ....glancing at the
closed door she sighed
Mr jahan looked at bakht .. you know he is doing all this
delibrately? His voice was serious
I know and I came prepared for the worst so don't worry
.. she gave him a assuring nod making him sigh   I have
mastered to hide my emotions ... She looked at window
Mr jahan pat her head ... Child he's my son I know him
well he will attack you where it stings the most

He points towards her posessive side …he knew well what his son is upto

Bakht smiled .. all that matters for me is his well being

Mr jahan left the room and Bakht sighed …for crying out loud she still love that idiot

She showered and changed and decided to head out   Only to find malika coming out of Sid's room …   Hii doctor malika stretched her hands …she adjusts her skinny nighty shyly making bakht cringe at the sight Calm down …calm down….she chanted in her head n

noded feeling herself taking deep breaths

Making her way to shams sahil room she found it empty Where are these monkeys?

The dinning table was filled with bakht's fav dishes   She was stunned to find everyone there …louis come up to her offering her a smile

Welcome back cupcake …he side hugged her making the girl chuckle

That's my pancake … Sahil shouted on shams n Zayn who ignored him n divided the pancake in two

Bro have it …Zayn gave choclate syrup to shams who grinned

Sahil look at zoya for help who immediately smacked shams n Zayn n snatched the pancake

Aww ..my teddy she cooed him cutting his air supply making Fahad frown n he pulled his heavy wife off him

Shaking her head Bakht too joined them but a maid came calling her

Dr …. Boss wants u to bring his breakfast . Bakht look at everyone …

Louis n Blake groaned …Fahad frowned while sahil shams n Zayn were too busy in pancake fight …zoya was glaring the poor orange juice

Bakht rolled her eyes and went to there boss den

Entering in the dark room she frowned ..but than roll her eyes

Does he think she is still afraid of dark?

Ohh plzz! You are .. her inner voice again poked making her groan

Placing the tray she opened the curtains earning a groan

Close

And click the door was closed and Bakht closed her eyes

Uh huh … It's not good not at all good !

Chapter 22

She looked at him and took the tray and gave her hand to
him to sit

Ignoring her help he stubbornly tried to sit by himself

She watched him rolling her eyes

Just how stubborn this men is

Huh … look who's speaking she mentally kicked her inner
voice

I don't have a whole day can we …. She spoke
professionally earning a glare from him   Call
my maliaka she will help me ..

Ouch! That hurts   Yeah
fine!

Bakht composed herself and turned to go hiding the tears

She returned huffing …your fiance is not here

She emphasised on fiance making him stiff

Nodding he let her help him …she bent down supporting
him his face inches away from hers

His hot breaths fanning on her neck …all those familiar
sensations ran in her body

She put the spoon near his mouth making him frown

I am not eating this …he whinned making bakht want to
smack him

It's in ur chart … You have to eat to get healthy sooner he
ignored her completely looking other side

She knew he won't budge and she needs to do something
to make him eat

Fine do whatever you want .. he still didn't acknowledged her presence

Sighing she adjusted pillows around his arms and left the room

He took a deep breath …his hands were itching to touch those silky hairlocks

You know …shams started earning everyone's attention

What? Zayn butt in intrested while Bakht n Sahil ignored him knowing well it's something absurd n useless

I have done a research …he declared

Bro you are a scientist …Zayn chirped earning a smack from zoya

That's researcher … she rolled her eyes   That's same …Zayn scoffed

So? What did u reasearched Blake ignored Zayn n zoya n looked at shams

There's an I love you at the end of family …shams announced

Frowning Fahad raised an eyebrow … What?

You see it's FAMILY last three ily is I love you   …he stated making Zayn n zoya snicker …Fahad facepalm himself while Blake glared him

Are u zayn's twin? Blake growled but Sahil heard it

Does Zayn too eats a lot? He innocently asked making everyone burst in laughter

Days were passing in blur and now it was time for Kabir's therapy sessions to start

He had irritated ..annoyed and hurt Bakht a lot these days Priotizing malika over her …getting all touchy with malika in front of her just to see the hurt in her eyes   As usual here he was throwing another tantrum

I am not going to do this shit …he roared making malika
flinch while Bakht roll her eyes   Done?
She calmly asked enraging him
Excusme ..you can't talk back with him .. if he's saying
he won't do it let it be
Mam .. I am doing my job Bakht calmly replied her   Eh?
Who are u even to order us? Don't forget we are paying
you hefty amount she keeps on insulting bakht but bakht
kept on gazing him who had turned his face   Stop came
a roar of jay …he had witnessed the vile women insulting
his baby princess
Clenching his fist he glared his brother …miss malika
…you are noone to disrespect her
You want to know her worth? She is the best
physiotherapist of dubai
You should thank her to be here …but nevermind …u can
do hell with yourself n your fiance he spat looking at his
brother
Taking bakht's hand in his he left the room leaving malika
n kabir
She turned to Kabir …baby you saw that bitch she sat
beside him who looked at her with bloodshot eyes
Just shut up …shut the fuck up n get out he yelled making
her gulp …he was shaking in anger
I said out …he screamed making her gasp n she left
Closing his eyes he pull his iPad checking the cctv
She was sitting in lawn looking at the trees …he sighed in
relief atleast she's not crying
But what he saw next boiled his blood …Jay came with
two cups n handed her one n even hugged her kissing her
temple and she giggled

Throwing the iPad in rage he closed his eyes taking deep breaths

Fuck! His eyes shot open and he wanted to kill someone right now   Precisely himself for hurting her …his carazon

Chapter 23

———◆———

Excusme ….shams called the nurse who just entered along dr micheal

Yes

Do u have a map? He seriously enquired

What? No …why would I have a map ? Is it a geography class …she sassed

Uh no ….. Actually I need the way to you he shyly said

The nurse glared him ….creep muttering she left

Shams turned dramatically .. ohh she's going to turn
Someone did turn but it was a grinning Zayn

Yukkksss ….shams made a disgusting face while Zayn was laughing like a hyena

It's been 1 month and kabir was much better now …he had stopped hurting her anymore

He does his exercise without showing any tantrum much to bakht's relief

Boss you are all set to walk in few days …micheal announced grinning while he only noded

With the help of stick …Kabir was walking in the lawn with bakht beside him

Great job dr bakht micheal gave bakht a greatful smile to which she smiled back

That's my work doctor …she dismissed the topic

That's all because of my prayers ..malika dramatically fanned herself

Yeah the one you do while Pedicure and facial …Jay mumbled making bakht chuckle

Sid glared his brother …in this one month Bakht hasn't spoken much with him …she only did her job but she's been really close to Jay n even micheal

Okay than …miss shefali can u plz assist dr bakht for further tests

The girl noded n turned to bakht who smiled warmly at her

It was next day when everyone including Kabir was doing breakfast

Bakht who just descended down ready to go out passed when Jay stopped her

Bakht …

Yes

Where are you going ? This catched Kabir's attention

Umm …I will be back soon she muttered lowly

What the fuck? The growl left louis mouth

Bakht too hault and looked at him among others   What? Kabir snapped annoyed

The fuck u don't know louis gritted playing the vedio The jahan heir all ready to be hitched with his secret fiance Wedding bells for Kabir jahan after getting secretly engaged with love of his life

Boss ? Blake asked flabbergasted I …I don't know Kabir was too confused who can do this

The news lines were enough to break her heart

  Excuse me ….muttering she dashed out of the house but damn these tears

What the actual fudge is happening here? Maya barged in kabir's room startling the guys

K …she screeched …I mean malika n u …ewww …she was ready to puke

Ok maya …we got u …Jay sighed

Kabir rubbed his temple …this all is malika's deed n now she's not here

But , he's also bothered with the fact that it's 9 in the night and Bakht hasn't return   As if cue …Blake's phone rang

Hello cupcake….yeah …he look at Sid who acted nonchalant

Fine …take care ..don't roam out late alright take care

Bakht will be back tomorrow she's with her friends

Who? Before kabir could realise he blurts

Before blake could say …ohh is she on date with that micheal guy .. hell she is enjoying .. Zayn squeeled dramatically

Blake frowned …she's with amy but seeing the mischief in zayn's eyes he played along

Yeah …yeah… both the boys smirked looking at the pissed off Kabir

Bakht returned to mansion next evening she needed time to fix herself

She was going inside when she saw him walking in lawn with his stick and a ciggerate

Frowning she made her way towards him

U arnt allowed to smoke…he turned to her and smirked

Where were u? He ignored her question n moved towards her

I was with my friends …she stated confused she had informed them already than why is he asking

Ohh …that lover boy huh? So …enjoyed the date ? Or I may say ….enjoyed the night with that Dr of urs   Bakht was horrified with the accusations w..hat?

Giving her a disgusting look he turned to go but stumble instinctively Bakht caught his arm

Don't fucking touch me …he roared making her flinch Go away …go n enjoy with that lover…fuck him all u want …I don't give …but she cut him off with a slap Tears spilled out of her eyes …u disgust me kabir …u disgust me

Seeing her tears something burnt inside him before they could say anything a frantic Fahad came out

Bakht …bakht..zoya …she …labour …he panted Ohh god! Fahad we need to rush hospital Bakht instructed him wiping her tears she run to her best friend who needs her now.

Chapter 24

Fahad was pacing in hospital corridor massaging his temples

Bakht came out and all the guys launch on her

What happened?   Is zee ok?

Baby …how's baby?

Guys calm down … Bakht smiled zoya n her baby boy is all healthy and chirpy

Giving a hug to Bakht …Fahad dashed inside   There zoya was she gave him a weak smile …and a thumbs up making him chuckle

His eyes are on me …Zayn chirped making fahad frown Rubbish … He's on me afterall he's my son he proudly announced

Zee …Blake ignored Zayn's and fahad's whinning … What's the name of this rabbit?

Zoya looked at Bakht …n gesture her to come

Bakht …she nudged her best friend …making bakht smile hanzal …Bakht announced earning hoots

Welcome to the clan hanzal …Zayn jumped and landed stomping on Blake's foot making him cry in pain   You buffoon get away!

Shefali was coming out with amy when shams spotted her She made a face seeing him ..

Excusme…shams had the big heart eyes

What? She snapped

Can u plz kick me ? Shams grinned

What why? Shefali frowned

Plzz …pretty plz …he pleaded

Shrugging …she kicked him making him yelp Yes! I am not dreaming you are here he cried dramatically making her roll her eyes

Creep …muttering she dashed away but shams was standing there with a stupid grin

Dad … Kabir was shocked hearing his father   Mr jahan didn't budge … do as I say

The hell …he roared … U want me to fucking marry that girl

He was seething …his dad had ordered him to make it official with malika

Yes ..I want you to not make any scene now …also u are fine now u can walk so bakht is going back he announced giving him another shock

2 weeks …it's been 2 weeks she has last spoke to him

…all the time either Zayn or Blake or Jay was with her Cutting all the chances of him to speak with her ..and over that the guilt

He had talked to micheal few days back n he informed him that he's on medical camp

That means she was right …he was already pissed with himself with the gutter he spoke to her

And now this …malika n him …sighing he closed his eyes

Mr jahan was in his study when Bakht entered making the men smile

Your work is done …he informed Bakht making her smile sadly

Thanku …she sat opposite to him

Beta what are u upto? Mr jahan was curious

Bakht smirked … Nothing ..just wondering about this malika

I should just break her jaw …she mumbled

Mr jahan smiled …this little warrior is on a mission

Alleeeleeeleeeeee ….allalallalala …Zayn was jumping making faces entertaining baby hanzal

Shams frowned and straighten Zayn… Let's show him dance

Grinning the boys started …zayn's hand on shams waist doing couple dance

Zoya burst in laughter along Bakht n Fahad

Sahil who was eating his chips looks up … Are u guys going to kiss too? He innocently asked making shams jump

Ewwww

Ewwwww

Both the guys were now standing at feet distance still horrified with the kiss idea

Bakht came back to her room when she saw malika entering Kabir's room in a lingerie

Smiling she winked at bakht …u know pre engagement celebration

Bakht noded n entered her room n that was it

The tears spilled and she cried her heart out

Just get out …and with that kabir closed the door on malika's face he leaned on door   What has he done?

With her

With them

His ego and her stubborness had destroyed them.

Chapter 25

———◆———

Putting the locket securely around her neck Bakht smiled seeing herself in the mirror

Today is hanazal's welcome party and his engagement Taking a deep breath she stepped out she surely will need a lot of courage today

Spotting zoya with her baby boy hanzel and Fahad Bakht smiled

They are family goals !

Bakht looked for the boys who were nowhere

She went to Sahil who was looking handsome in his tux

Ohh my sweet cups my sahil is looking so cute ..Bakht cooed her baby brother hugging or more like crushing him

Making Sahil frown ... Leave me can't breath he struggled out

The boy was crushed in another hug by shams   Aaww my butterfly .. how handsome you became .. shams squeeled like a girl

Bakht rolled her eyes and stomp on his foot

Ouch ouch! Mumma ... he screamed making bakht frown

They were bickering when the guys scooted away to food leaving her alone

The music started and Bakht who was drinking her drink stopped

Closing her eyes bakht remember there first kiss ...how his lips mould against hers

As in cue he entered and stopped searching someone in the croud and his eyes stopped on her   She looked away from him ….

Go and fuck him all u want ...

How   was   ur   date   huh?

Loverboy eh?

Don't fucking touch me

His accusing words rang in her mind making her take a sharp breath

She turned away and gulped the soar drink …   Sensing her discomfort zoya and Fahad came by her side and zoya hugged her ..

He watched her now talking to Jay …she's looking absolutely amazing   As always !

Sensing an intense gaze she turned and there eyes met .. He remembers how she left him …lied to him …made him heartless how he missed her every fucking day and night how his heart ache seeing her so close yet so far … and closed his eyes overwhelmed with the emotions   A traitor tear leaked her eyes but he noticed it and clenched his fists

She still loves him it's clear as water than what's stopping her?

The question made him frustrated with himself ..

She spotted a happy malika and reminiscences how she is always around him …going in his room …are they happy?

Has he moved on ?

Malika saw him gazing Bakht and in fury she marched towards her untangling her leg in front of her making bakht disbalance

She was about to fall but he held her firmly …

Looking up she find him inches away …his hands on her elbow while hers on his bicep …

She quickly moved back but he didn't looked away instead keep looking at her …

She turned and went away leaving him alone ….again
He gulped the bitter alchohal his eyes bloodshot red

His heart was bleeding …his mind frustrated his body numb

Taking another drink he gulped it making himself slightly tipsy …

Chapter 26

He looked at her who was silently sitting beside Jay

So she doesn't mind him seeing with someone else huh?

He looked at her with bloodshot eyes and grabbed

malika harshly making her hiss …

His fingers were digging in her naked waist …he wasn't
in his senses …malika took it as a chance and starts
kissing his face n neck.

But seeing him looking at her she's knows he's doing all
this to hurt her

Now when he look at malika standing with him all he
could see was her in malika

Alcohal has hazed his mind ..he looked at her intensely
imagining Bakht with him

Her heart brakes looking at him gazing another women
with so much emotions

Not able to take it anymore she went out wiping away the
tears …

He could feel himself breaking apart along her

His heart is breaking within her

His carazon

While the guys along zoya n maya stood in remorse

Why God tests those who love?

Chapter 27

Kabir looked the way she left the party and his own eyes burned

Taking deep breaths he left malika with a jerk

She cling in his arms again making him frustrated

Suddenly the hall was silent and gunshots were heard

Zayn along the boys were immediately alert and took out there guns

But ... There own men's betrayed them and gunshots were heard ...then entered the main villan

Noah

Hello my friend ...long tym huh? He smirked at kabir Now comeon ..smile before you die because ...tsk ..he looked at his right

Zayn along the other guys Were held by Noah's men Zoya was clutching hanzel to her chest while maya was beside her

I see ..u get some beautiful ladies huh ...he gazed at maya from top to bottom

U flithy bastard ...louis growled making him snicker Ohh .... The great commander Blake ...must say your sister was a fiesty one eh ..

Blake froze hearing this ...he was wriggling like a bull making Noah laugh evily

But alas..before I could have her that J person took her he scowled

Malika who stood beside Kabir suddenly pushed him away taking his gun

Noah again laughed …and malika stood beside him clinging on him

Ohh bitch I missed u …he kissed her making her laugh a flirty one

The guys were shocked …and kabir was silent all the time
Now …now , let me tell u something u know this darling of mine was here

You remember how she came in your life ?

And kabir remembered the fateful day 1 year back
Flashback
The Jahan's had a fight and in that war John one of there trusted men died

He had a daughter Mr jahan wanted to take care of her
They found malika in his house and upon confronting she confirmed to be daughter of John

She acted like she is suffering and is scared so the Jahan's took her with them …. Which they did to compensate
And she starts living with them but noone ever got a positive vibe from her

Fb ends

I must say darling this Kabir here is whipped with that witch…she spat angrily

I tried to seduce him but he …he always had that name
Noah snickered …it's not his fault that Chick was….he dreamily said but before that a punch land on his face
Kabir saw red …dare you take her name n I will rip your lungs out he growled

Malika stab him on his back making him stumble

Now …lets get over this Noah pull out his gun wiping his blood and points to Kabir

Gunshot was heard and everyone froze

Dare you touch my men … bakht stood
there with a cold expression

Her aura oozing confidence …the gun in her hand was
pitch black in color

Everyone was too shocked to react while Noah cried
clutching his leg

She came forward taking confident strides and put her
pointed hill on his wound making him yelp

Noah huh? Long tym ….she smirked than looked at
malika who gulped

Now …now …she clutched her hairs…u dare touch
what's mine girl she growled on her face and pushed her
on floor

Zoya and Zayn whistle making Fahad roll his eyes
Taking out her knife she cut malika's palms making her
cry

That's for touching him bitch …then she stabbed her legs
…that's for coming here in the first place

Then she took out her gun and shoot her arms without
flinching

That's for trying to harm my baby hanzel …malika was
half conscious by now and everyone gulped seeing the
ruthlessness of Bakht

Then she turned to Noah n leaned on his level ..u wanted
to know who took laila ?

Blake snapped towards her …standing up she smirked
Well that was me …it always was me …J she turned to
Kabir who was standing like a statue

A whisper left his mouth …jahan?

She shot Noah in between his head and then malika simultaneously

Everybody was too stunned to react …

Then she looked around the people who were holding the guys were dead and Bakht smirked

Ok shams …come out she shouted

A grinning shams along with sahil and Mr jahan came out

So how was the show guys? Shams grinned

Silence

 After a pregnant pause ….

It was fun-fooking-tastic and with that zoya jumped on bakht making her giggle

Chapter 28

Bakht eyes wander to him who was standing there like a statue his gauge on back was oozing blood

She quickly ran towards him and made him sit down all the time she didn't look at his face knowing well about his piercing gaze

After bandaging him she turned but he held her hand

 How? …his voice was gruff and thick with emotions ..taking deep breath she freed her hands

Mr jahan saw his son and knew well that bakht is not going to forgive him anytime soon for his stupidity so he came forward

I was the one who helped her leave Russia …he announced making everyone gasp

Kabir was shell shocked on hearing that he had begged his father multiple tims to find her n all he said was it's of no use

Her leaving back then was all planned he remembered that day

It was before that night when they came to know about Noah being in Australia

Bakht had received a call from Noah and he informed her about sahil her brother and that if she wants him she should kill Kabir

After crying for hours … helplessly she dialled mr Jahan's number .

He too was shocked but he made her understand that she should not keep herself weak her parents were one proud people and now it's time for her to understand her power So he planned all this …she left Russia and after that she was trained for 10 months …

Her first attack was Anderson who had sahil with him Saving her brother who was brutally beaten n drugged she was more admanent to take revenge

From that day she killed mercilessly without flinching and that day she swore to protect Jahan's because they are only people left whoom she calls hers

Coming here was not a plan but faith brought her here and after seeing Kabir's condition that day she realised that someone doesn't want him to get back to normal ..his medicines had some blunder

So she planned to be here and kabir made her work easy himself

On keeping close watch she was suspicious on malika and her doubts got confirmed

She disclosed this to Mr jahan and then they planned this It was Mr jahan himself who leaked the news and as usual malika got trapped and Noah overconfident

Mr jahan sighed finishing the story …

Bakht turned to Blake and smiled…she looked at shams who dialled a number

After half an hour amy entered with a girl

She looked nervous and was seeing everyone with scared eyes

Seeing bakht she ran to her n clutched her hand

Laila …Bakht softly called the petite girl and she looked at her with her big brown eyes

She took her to Blake …laila he is your brother

Laila looked at blake …same brown eyes …the resemblance of features were same

Brother   …she whispered making blake tearful

Brother…she again repeated making blake chock and he nod in yes

Lailly …he softly called hopping the girl will recognize him …he use to call her that

Brother? She did …she did recognise and hugged her brother crying in his arms

Everyone got emotional while Zayn..zoya and shams were bawling there eyes …crying like kids

Ok kids … No more crying go to your rooms n rest we will talk later .. Mr jahan smiled

Without sparing kabir any glance Bakht went away

She cried her heart out in shower …it was when she got ready for bed her door was knocked

Opening the door she came face to face with him

He gave her his charming smile …

hey

Not again !

Chapter 29

Blake room door was knocked making him groan from sleep

It must be Zayn …cursing Zayn he opened the door ready to shout but the sight made his sleep flew away   Amal was standing there with a bored expression

You? What's this disaster doing here

Pushing him and ignoring his question she made her way inside and made herself comfortable on his bed

Frowning he turned raising an eyebrow …

I can't sleep there …she pointed towards her room which is just opposite to his   So? He was irritated

I am sleeping here …she announced and snuggled in his duvet

Are you nuts ? He growled coming to her

Shh … Amy is with laila and I can't sleep alone so …she trailed and he shut up

Yeah …. For his baby sister laila …sighing he closed the door

Don't dare u sleep on bed amal threw his pillow on him

I am not dying to sleep here anyways …he rolled his eyes

Go die on couch she ordered smugly

Bakht stood there dumbstruck why on muffins he is here?

What are u doing here ? Bakht asked in a clipped tone

I …he started but seeing her cold expression gulped   If you don't have anything to say so kindly let me sleep ..I have to travel and with that she banged the door   Kabir rubbed his back …

fuck this is difficult …

The next morning Bakht came down and found everyone on breakfast table

Come Bakht …Jay called her making the girl smile

She sat between Zayn and shams and immediately regretted Baby that's for hanzel …Fahad tried to explain zoya who was eating hanzels carelek (baby food)

So ? It's tasty plus I am teaching him to share ….zoya shrugged

A soft giggle was heard and everyone snapped towards a giggling laila and smiling sahil

Sensing everyone's attention both went stiff …

They are best friends …amy exclaimed

Yeah and they leave me all alone like what the duck? Shams cried dramatically

But noone was feeling sympathatized towards him making him whine more

Uh … Bakht started gaining everyone's attention   Now that everything is ok I want to go back …. I wanna return los Angels to my old life

Kabir chocked on his food …making louis chuckle glaring him he looked at his father pleading for help

Sure… Whatever makes you happy my child he smiled making Kabir want to hit his own head somewhere

Everyone was sulking in living room when zoya said …

Correction : zoya shouted

Ok guys ! I am still alive ..don't make pig face   Now comeon let's plan something for bakhti she sang in ears making him groan

Zee … .we got u stop shouting Blake said making zoya pout

Go hurry search ideas …shooo …she ordered making them roll there eyes

Everyone was thinking when laila spoke …you guys can spend time with her she will b happy

Blake grinned …my princess is so smart

That she is Zayn agreed grinning but Blake glared him Zayn scoffed .. she's a sister chill!

Okay then … Let bakhti come back from hospital than we are gonna rock   Call Amy and amal as well …louis suggested smirking at blake and Zayn

Kabir was pacing in his room …he has to talk to her but he knew well that angry bakht can be dangerous

Scratch dangerous …angry bakht is scary !

And the mighty Kabir jahan is afraid of her being hurt!

Chapter 30

Bakht came back but frown finding pin drop silence in living room

Bhooooommmmm ….and there they are with party poopers …the whole room was decorated with lights and music was playing

It's your farewell party from us … Shams grinned   Zoya hit his head … You are also going with her n roll her eyes

Bakht smiled looking at the people who cared for her so much

And then they start the party …eating …laughing …dancing …

Bakht was dancing with micheal as he was also invited

Amal dragged Blake blakmailing him

Sahil and laila were softly dancing

Whereas shams and Zayn were doing funny jumping which they called dance

Kabir who just came back saw the party going on with a frown

He smiled looking at Fahad who was playing with hanzel

His eyes darted to her and immediately his smile was wiped off

Micheal's hand was all over her back while he was too close to her face

The last nail hit the coffin when she threw her head back n laughed while micheal tap her nose

This is it

He marched towards the music system and smashed it on ground

Everyone was too stunned looking at him who was oozing danger

Grabbing Bakht in a death grip he yanked her away from micheal

Ignoring her wriggling and yelling for Fahad to stop him … he Dragged her to his room

Fahad was going when zoya stopped him …let them be she squeezed his hand assuringly

Yanking Bakht inside Kabir locked the door and threw his jacket somewhere

Bakht gulped looking the vein throbbing on his neck

He's madly angry

She huffed and tried to open the door but no avail

Turning she found him sitting on couch now   What the …she started but he stride towards her and forcefully made her sit on couch

Enough …now we will talk … Enough of your tantrums Silence

After a long silence he took her hands in his

Carazon …I am sorry …I am sorry for being a jerk …for saying that shit things to u

He took a deep breath …I was already mad on myself bcz of that bitch who disrespected you and then me being a douchbag said all those things   He kissed her hands …I m sorry

She looked at him teary eyed …u didn't trust me her voice was low n meak

Kabir sighed …I …I was too much jaelous to think straight that tym

I am sorry plz …his voice was thick with emotions
Bakht looked at him he was looking like a zombie

Dark circles …dishieved hairs …messy clothes   And at
this moment she knew that it was not his fault entirely
She leaned and pa

Pecked his lips …sorry she mumbled making him shock

I shouldn't have left .. I should have talked with you ..
toldyou everything .. fear of loosing you made my senses
numb .. I am sorry for all the pain and sufferings … He
sat there gazing at her beautiful face

Smiling she again pecked his lips ..one two three …he
groaned and took her lips in a smoothing kiss .. Pouring
all the pain … sufferings and longings of these years   I
love u bakht

I love u too Kabir .. I always had ..always will

Both smiled and finally they were at peace after the long
battle

He realised what she must have been through when he left
her uninformed , she realised her fear of him being in
harm had snatched five years from them

But it's mistakes and distance that keeps the relationship
stronger

And atlast …love wins …. .

Epilogue

———◆———

3 yrs later

Gunshots ….gunshots …..gunshots ….

The men looked at the source where the gunshots was heard and sighed

Guess someone's here …again

He made a face and tug his gun looking at his left he glared the other one who was smirking

Louis was totally enjoying the rivalry between his boss and his wife

A groaning Blake came to the garden …boss 3 vase …2 couches …2 teddy beer are being shot by your wife Louis burst in laughter making blake chuckle … Kabir rubbed his back nervously

He's late by 2 hours and his wife who is pregnant will now sue him alive

Entering in the living room he was attacked by a flying viper …than a curse …

U …piece of plastic …flying slippers ….u son of biscuit …flying stool ….you .. pig ….you idiot …I ..hate you …and then she starts crying making everyone panick No no sister don't … Plz don't cry Zayn was himself about to cry

Plz bakhtii break his head but don't cry ….zoya groaned banging her head on sofa than hissed in pain

 Carazon …baby …see I have ice cream Kabir came forward cautiously making her pout

With her big tummy and red face she was looking absolutely beautiful n cute

Okay …baby see I am sorry I really am he cooed her making her look at him with a pout

You are really sorry right? She confirmed now carrasing his bearded jaw …this is what is happening nowadays one minute she's all macho on him and other she is all lovey dovey

Pregnancy hormones eh?

Everyone relaxed and got back to there rooms …   Kabir picked his wife who is now busy with ice cream n kissed her nose making her giggle

It's been 2 years they are married and she's 7 months pregnant now

These 2 years are the most blissful years of his life ..they fought ..they bickered but at night they would cuddle and all fights will be vanished

Covering Bakht with a duvet he changed in his night clothes and than took her swollen feets massaging them making her relax and smile in sleep

Kissing her belly he talked to his princess …he's sure that it's a girl n he's going to make sure that his girl will be truly treated as a princess

Hii baby …he kissed her belly again

Hii pea .. you didn't get afraid of the gunshots right? He placed his hand on her belly n feel a kick making him grin

His baby girl is dad's girl truly!

Baby ..dad got a new wardrobe for u ..we will surprise mumma he grinned imagining the all cute stuffs he had selected today while he was in office

Nowadays all he is thinking is about his baby n his carazon

Cuddling her in his arms he slept dreaming about there prefect family

Blake entered his room and looked at his phone   No calls

Amal is upset with him …reason is still a mystery   He still can't believe that he can fell for someone like amal

Maybe … opposite attracts n in his case it's totally true

Sighing he call the stubborn girl call who immediately cut the call

She was definitely on the phone just to cut the call …chuckling he lay down thinking about the ways he can coax his dove

Shefali was coming out of the hospital when a running shams joined her walking side by side

Arnt you tired? He grinned making her roll her eyes

Cheesy …but a smile erupt on her face ..

Why? She snapped as usual

U know u have been running away from too long he again grinned making her stop

Turning to him she stared him …coming close she whispered maybe I like running so you can be troubled

And like that she ran away laughing leaving him there stunned and speechless …

Zayn and Amy both know about the feelings they share but …

One is bound to responsibility of her sister and other is bound to promise made with his love   (They arnt aware about Blake n amal)

Only time can heal these two longing hearts

Life is a trial …and trials arnt meant to be easy remember that!

The End